This is a Magabala Book
LEADING PUBLISHER OF ABORIGINAL AND
TORRES STRAIT ISLANDER STORYTELLERS.
CHANGING THE WORLD, ONE STORY AT A TIME.

First published 2022. Reprinted 2022, 2023
Magabala Books Aboriginal Corporation
1 Bagot Street Broome, Western Australia
Website: www.magabala.com Email: sales@magabala.com

Magabala Books receives financial assistance from the Commonwealth Government through the Australia Council, its arts advisory body. The State of Western Australia has made an investment in this project through the Department of Local Government, Sport and Cultural Industries. Magabala Books would like to acknowledge the support of the Shire of Broome, Western Australia.

Magabala Books is Australia's only independent Aboriginal and Torres Strait Islander publishing house. Magabala Books acknowledges the Traditional Owners of the Country on which we live and work. We recognise the unbroken connection to traditional lands, waters and cultures. Through what we publish, we honour all our Elders, peoples and stories, past, present and future.

This title is proudly supported by the ALIA Online Storytime program, through the Australian Government RISE Grants funding.

Printed in China by Everbest Printing
Packaged by Ballantyne Rawlins in collaboration with Magabala Books

The illustrations in this book were created with mixed media, comprising painting, printmaking and digital collage.

ISBN 9781922613769

A catalogue record for this book is available from the National Library of Australia

Department of Local Government, Sport and Cultural Industries

For all the language learners making their way home, and for David Wilkins and Denise Angelo for helping on the way.

J.S.

JASMINE SEYMOUR is a Dharug woman belonging to the Burubiranggal people, descended from Maria Lock and Yarramundi. She is the mother to two boys.

Jasmine is the author / illustrator of *Baby Business*, winner of the 2020 CBCA Best New Illustrator Award and is also the author of the 2020 Prime Minister's Literary Award winning children's title, *Cooee Mittigar*, illustrated by Leanne Mulgo Watson.

Jasmine has a masters degree in Indigenous languages education and is a Dharug language teacher and language activist. As a researcher Jasmine collaborated with Grace Karskens on the Real Secret River project and was a co-curator for the Dyarubin exhibition at the State Library of New South Wales.

Jasmine is the secretary of the Da Murrytoola Aboriginal Education Consultancy Group (AECG) and is a primary school teacher in Western Sydney. This is Jasmine's fourth book with Magabala.

Open your heart to Country

JASMINE SEYMOUR

Magabala Books

Open your heart
to Country.
Let place soothe
your lonely feet.
Yarramundi Maria Lock John Lock Hannah Lock Elsie Morley Laurel Douglas Stephen Seymour Jasmine Seymour

Ngiyini Ngurrawa – You are on Country.

Walama ngurragu – Return home.

Welcome home lost children,
to land singing you back home.

Listen to its language.
Learn how to speak its song.

Ngara Ngurrangai dhalangu – Listen to the language of Country.

Let it wrap you in a bed of bark,
back where you came from.

Ngiyini Ngurrabirang – You are of Country

Your skin might have many names.
You might be far from home.

Warami. Budyari naady'unya – Where are you from? Good to see you.

Dabuwamilyi Ngurragu – Paint up for Country.

Long-ago-stories will cover you.
Listen. Love. Learn.

Move through the smoke,
let it cover you.

Garrimalyi gadyala – Cleanse yourself with smoke.

Dance with bare feet on the ground.

Dhangurraya! Let's dance!

Open your heart to Country.

Sleep in its emu Milky Way.
Mariyanga yudibanya burawa – The emu will guide you across the sky.

Banga baranyiin baribugu ...

Paddle from yesterday to tomorrow ...

Swim in its river of stars.

walamagulang ngiyini ngurragu – to return to your home.

On Country where you belong.

Open your heart to Country.
Let place soothe your lonely feet.

Welcome home lost children,
To land singing you back home.

Listen to its language.
Learn how to speak its song.

Let it wrap you in a bed of bark,
Back where you come from.

Your skin might have many names.
You might be far from home.

Long ago stories will cover you.
Listen. Love. Learn.

Move through the smoke,
Let it cover you.

Dance with bare feet on the ground.

Open your heart to Country.
Sleep in its emu Milky Way.

Swim in its river of stars.

On Country where you belong.

Ngiyini Ngurrawa
You are on Country.

Walama ngurragu
Return home.

Ngara Ngurrangai dhalangu
Listen to the language of Country.

Ngiyini Ngurrabirang
You are of Country.

Warami! Budyari naady'unya
Where are you from? Good to see you.

Dabuwamilyi Ngurragu
Paint up for Country.

Garrimalyi gadyala
Cleanse yourself with smoke.

Dhangurraya!
Let's dance!

Mariyanga yudibanya burawa
The emu will guide you across the sky.

Banga baranyiin baribugu …
Paddle from yesterday to tomorrow …

walamagulang ngiyiningai ngurragu
returning you to home.

This story is told in two languages, English and Dharug. Dharug language has been spoken by people who have lived across the Sydney basin for thousands of years.

Readers will notice there are Dharug words on each page. The English words alongside them translate what those words say and show us how the ideas in the main English story would be expressed by Dharug speakers.

Because no two languages ever follow exactly the same sentence patterns, and all cultures express concepts and ideas in their own way, we learn a lot about how different societies think when we listen to and learn new languages. By reading the Dharug words told with their own English translations, you will 'hear' this story with Dharug ears.

Dharug people are working hard to reawaken our language. It is hard work to learn a language and even harder to first go back in history to find it. How wonderful to learn the deep roots of our language story. A story that has been disrupted but never forgotten.

The workings of Dharug are different to English. Our language LOVES putting endings on words — lots of them. You might notice that Dharug sentences have fewer words than the English translations. That's because Dharug word endings replace lots of the little words English loves such as is, a, the, and to, among others.

Dharug has its own spelling system for its own sounds. Most letters make roughly the same sounds as English, but there are a few tricky ones.

dh like the *th* in father

ng just like in sa*ng*a (short for sandwich). Dharug words can start with this sound too.

dy the closest English sound is *jar*

rr is a trilled *r* sound like you might make when you are cold, and say, '*Brrrrr*'.

a like the sound in the word c*u*p. The *aa* used in some Dharug words is like the sound in f*a*ther.

u like the sound in p*u*t. When *uu* is used it sounds like the double '*oo*' in food.

i as in s*i*t. When *ii* is used it makes the sound as in s*ee*.